Lullaby for a Newborn King

A Christmas Story by **Józef Wilkoń** and **Hermann Moers**

Illustrated by **Józef Wilkoń**

Translated by **Rosemary Lanning**

North-South Books

New York

There was once a shepherd boy named Simon who could play the most beautiful music on his flute. When he took his sheep and goats to graze high on the mountainside, he always carried his flute with him and the sound of his playing could be heard for miles around. Simon's father and mother, Matthew and Elisa, could hear Simon's music in their hut far below. Sometimes it helped them forget how poor they were.

It was darkest night and Simon and his parents were asleep on their straw mattresses with their blankets pulled right up to their ears to protect them from the bitter cold.

As they slept, a bright light came streaming into the hut. The animals woke at once, raised their heads and gazed at the window.

Simon sat up and rubbed his eyes. He knew it couldn't be morning yet because the sheep were silent, not bleating as they always did at daybreak.

Then Matthew woke. He hadn't wanted to open his eyes at first because it would have meant letting go of a wonderful dream. But this strange, powerful light was too bright to be ignored.

Matthew ran to the window, and at once shouted, "Elisa! Drive the animals outside. The sky is on fire! If a spark lands on our roof, all will be lost."

Matthew climbed onto the roof of the hut. "Come down! Come down!" cried Elisa in horror. "The roof is too weak to bear your weight."

Matthew just stared at the sky, too dazzled to worry about his safety.

"A blazing star is coming towards us!" he shouted. "Simon, run to the wise man in the village and ask him what this means. The star must be a sign."

Simon set off for the village at great speed.

As Simon ran he could see a woman standing outside her hut with her head in her hands.

"This must be the end of the world," she moaned.

But further down the path people were dancing with joy. "The star means we will never be poor again," they said. "It's a *good* sign."

When Simon reached the house where the wise man lived there was already a crowd of people, all wanting to know the meaning of the dazzling star with the fiery tail.

The old man gazed at the sky for a long time. Then he turned, his eyes no longer dim with age but blazing with the brilliance of the star. In a ringing voice he told the waiting people: "The star tells of the birth of a long-awaited king. You must go and welcome him, and take him gifts. The star will lead you to him."

Simon hurried home to tell his parents of the birth of the new king.

Elisa carefully wrapped some of her best cheese to take to the king and they set out at once to follow the star. On the way other shepherds joined them, some bringing their animals in case the journey should be long. Suddenly Simon stopped. "I have forgotten to bring a present," he said, and turned to run back to the hut.

Simon searched and searched for something to give to the new king, but he couldn't find anything good enough. How could he greet a king with an old soup spoon? Or a cup with no handle? Or a fragment of broken mirror?

He began to cry. He hated to think he would be the only one with no gift. Then he remembered his flute.

"I will play him a tune!" he said, wiping away his tears. Simon picked up the flute and ran as fast as he could to catch up with the others.

At last the shepherds' journey came to an end. They had expected the star to lead them to a big town or to a rich man's dwelling. Instead the star had brought them to an old, tumbledown stable in the little town of Bethlehem.

"This can't be the right place," complained some of them. "Let's go home."

The shepherds approached the stable warily, uncertain of what they would find in such a place. But Simon stepped boldly up to the stable door. And there was Jesus, the newborn king, lying in a manger, on a bed of hay. Beside him were his mother Mary and his father Joseph, both exhausted from the difficult journey which had brought them to this humble shelter.

Jesus, the newborn king, began to cry. This cold, windy stable was no place for a baby, and perhaps he was afraid of all the people who had suddenly crowded in.

Mary lifted the baby from his crib and wrapped him in her cloak.

Everyone pressed forward, holding out their gifts to Jesus, calling to him, begging him to grant their requests. There was so much noise that Mary could not soothe her child.

Simon tiptoed closer and when he heard the new king crying he remembered his own gift. He nervously pulled his flute from his pocket and set it to his lips.

The tune that he played was new even to him and seemed to come from deep inside, drawn out by his wish to comfort the child.

There was no other sound in the stable. Everyone was listening to Simon's music. And as the last notes faded, the baby stopped crying and fell asleep. It was as if Simon's melody had wrapped him in a warm blanket, and shut out the cold of the night. Simon was happy. Jesus had accepted his gift, a lullaby for the newborn king.

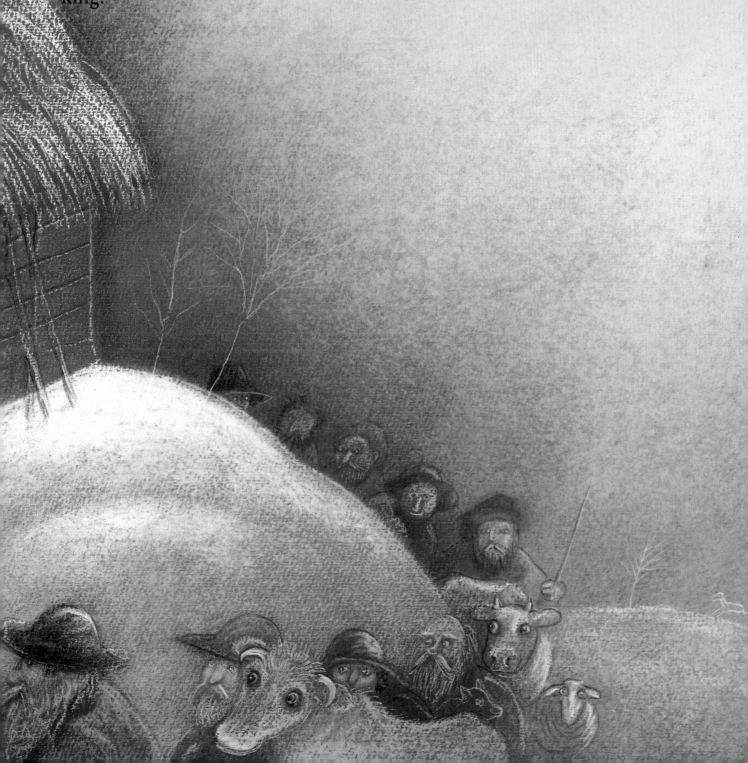